This Book Belongs
to

TOO GOOD To Be TRUE

in rhyme

by Aunt Mugg

All inquiries may be directed to:
Siloam Publishing Company
P.O. Box 174
Jarrettsville, Maryland 21084
(www.weezyswoods.com)

Thanks to my nephew Michael Stephen Zvonar III
for his artistic advice and technical assistance.

First Printing
Printed in the United States of America
ISBN 0-9668358-2-4

And as He passed by, He saw a man blind from birth.

And his disciples asked Him, saying, "Rabbi, who sinned, this man or his parents, that he should be born blind?"

Jesus answered, "It was neither that this man sinned nor his parents; but it was in order that the works of God might be displayed in him."

"We must work the works of Him who sent Me, as long as it is day; night is coming, when no man can work.

"While I am in the world, I am the light of the world."

When He had said this, He spat on the ground, and made clay of the spittle, and applied the clay to his eyes,

and said to him, "Go, wash in the pool of Siloam" (which is translated, Sent). And so he went away and washed, and came back seeing.

The neighbors therefore, and those who previously saw him as a beggar, were saying, "Is not this the one who used to sit and beg?"

Others were saying, "This is he," still others were saying, "No, but his is like him." He kept saying, "I am the one."

Therefore they were saying to him, "How then were your eyes opened?"

He answered, "The man who is called Jesus made clay, and anointed my eyes, and said to me, 'Go to Siloam and wash'; so I went away and washed, and I received sight."

(John 9:1-11)

“Hey Gus! Check this out!” cried Nutmeg with glee.
He held up a small magazine.
Gus peered intently and Nutmeg went on,
“Look here! You see what I mean?”

TOTALLY FREE
WON’T COST YOU A CENT
Bicycle, ten-speed, brand new

“What do you think?!”
Nutmeg squealed with delight.
“It sounds way too good to be true!”

"That's 'cause it probably *is*,"
Thought the frog,
Waking up from a long, groggy snooze.

"Sounds good to me!" answered Gus.
"What a *deal*!
Go for it! What can you lose?"

"What can you lose"
Thought the frog, drifting off
To a slumber unconscious and deep…
Where he once again lived
Through the nightmare that was
So real that he squirmed in his sleep.

Twenty-five years ago, life here was good…
In no way the frog felt deprived.
The frog was content in his day-to-day life,
Until…Maestro Flaco arrived.

Early one morning, it happened right here,
They came…and perhaps I should mention,
Campers were common; sometimes they passed through,
So Vladimir paid no attention.

But too bad for Vladimir, poor little frog,
Regrettably Maestro saw *him*.
Happily sunning himself on a rock,
Fresh from his cool morning swim.

Pulling out fingers, then snapping them back…
My goodness! What stretchable hands!
It was those fingers that caught Maestro's eye,
Elastic! Like long rubber bands!

The Maestro's assistant at once recognized
His sparkling eyeballs, and so…
Desperately Pepe, begged on his knees,
"Leave him be Maestro! LET'S GO!"

But Maestro ignored him and shook the frog's hands.
"Forgive me if I seem abrupt.
But I've got an offer you *just can't* refuse!

And Pepe, **please** don't interrupt!"

Glaring at Pepe, the Maestro went on. “I tell you, I said what I meant.
Come with me boy, and I’ll show you the world,
And Friend, it won’t cost you a cent.

“I’ll watch over you as you play night and day, and I’ll take you to Paris in June.
The sky’s *not* the limit…and maybe one day, we might even fly to the moon!”

Indeed, all this sounded too good to be true;
Vladimir just wasn't sure.
And seeing him weakening, Maestro moved in
And pressed on the frog all the more.

"Just one little item we mustn't forget…
A small legal detail. Don't fear.
But-once-you're-committed-you-won't-be-acquitted-it's-a-twenty-year-contract…

SIGN

… here."

So, shoving some papers right under his nose, he convinced the poor frog to comply.
The frog was naïve, so he wasn't aware of the gleam that was in Maestro's eye.

When he signed the contract, he had *no* idea
Just what it was that he'd done…
A trip 'round the world, a vacation of sorts…a scenery change.
It'd be *fun*. *(Proverbs 14:15)*

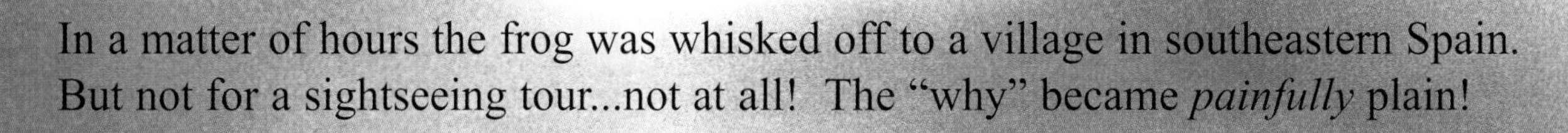

In a matter of hours the frog was whisked off to a village in southeastern Spain.
But not for a sightseeing tour...not at all! The "why" became *painfully* plain!

He was going to play on *something* all right, but it sure wasn't seesaws or swings!
It was a ***piano***…a **GRAND** one at that!
The frog had been tricked! Of all things!

"I told you you'd travel, and travel you shall," he said to his new protégé.
"Think of it! Cairo and Suva and Perth, with concerts and fame
everyday!

"Together we'll conquer the stars, my dear boy,
A partnership! That's you and me!
My greatest ambition? To play on the moon!
And we'll get there, just *trust me* and see!"

The view was fantastic; but not for the frog...a piano, four walls, that was all of it.
The castle was grand, but he might well have been
In Cleveland for all that *he* saw of it.

When Vladimir timidly asked if he could
See the Prado, the boss flipped his lid.
"The ***PRADO?!*** FORGET IT!
We won't have the time!
And anyway, that's in Madrid.
"I *said* you could play!
What **more** do you want?
Remember the contract you signed!"

But playing arpeggios, etudes and scales
Wasn't *quite* what the frog had in mind.

The Maestro was tough; he drilled that poor frog
All day and then on through the night.
Pepe watched helplessly feeling his pain,
But couldn't help, try as he might.

Pepe knew Vladimir just didn't have
The stamina of Señor Flaco.
The frog needed rest; it was days since he'd slept
And a week since he'd eaten gazpacho.

And so it went week after strenuous week. T'was months since the frog had a meal.
Vladimir timidly got up his courage
And made a pathetic appeal.

Are you INSANE?!?
There's **work** to be done!
Think practice! Think scales! Forget munchies!"

But Pepe took pity upon the poor frog
And slipped him a couple of cheese crunchies.

So
on
went
the
months;

The frog
had no sleep.

So much for
sightseeing
and trips.

His lids were so heavy, the boss propped them up
With toothpicks and used paper clips.

And true to his word, the Maestro watched over
The frog as he played night and day,

And all the while raving he'd be on the moon…
But how could this be? Who could say?

The idea was crazy, but so was the boss,
So maybe he *would* find a way…

And so it went year after year and the frog would never (it seemed) get a break.
In reaching for music, his toes touched the keys…oh goodness! A fatal mistake!

Not ten...but TWENTY! The Maestro's eyes gleamed.
"My boy!" *Now* we'll work 'til you drop!
With double the fingers, we'll work twice as hard!
From here we go straight to the top!"

"But first off there's something that has to be done in case something happens to you!
No point taking chances, we'll need to insure
Your fingers ***and*** all your toes too!"

So off to an agent in London somewhere,
Where they measured his fingers and toes.
And all the while tugging and stretching and just
Stopping short of beeping his nose.

"These are incredible! Marvelous toes! Amazing! Like nothing we've seen!
One million per toe, a fair price and so, insure twenty tootsies, Old Bean."

Well, ten long years later, the frog was prepared
To put on his very first show.
Now came the traveling…and with it the sights!
And he'd earned it…yes, rightfully so.

The frog gathered courage and asked the big man
If he might have a little diversion.
He timidly showed him a travel brochure
With a typical tourist excursion.

Maestro told Pepe,
"He wants to sightsee.
That's *your* job.
You see that he does."

Then Pepe got postcards
And set them all up
So Vladimir knew where he was.

Ephesus, Jarrettsville, Agra and Thule,
Montevideo and Rome…

Everything four walls could offer he saw from Melbourne, Australia to Nome.

Airport to concert hall, then to hotel; the schedule was grueling and brutal.
Pepe so wished he could help the poor frog, but any attempts would be futile.
(Proverbs 29:7)

For Pepe to get the poor frog all alone was impossible…my what a plight!
Maestro watched Vladimir just like a hawk, never letting him out of his sight.

Autograph sessions…

Recordings…

And more…

Quite frankly, the frog was in deep.
Maestro made sure there was time for it all,
With, of course, the exception of sleep.

Now everything Vladimir'd done up 'til now was merely to get him "in tune"
For one major concert; his last one on earth,
Then after?
T'was
on
to
the...

MOON!

This was *the* concert! The show of all shows!
This show was the means to the end.
An art exhibition-recital combined and
The richest of rich would attend.

Success at the show assured Maestro one thing beyond international fame;
The earth was just peanuts...the moon would be next
With *intergalactic* acclaim!

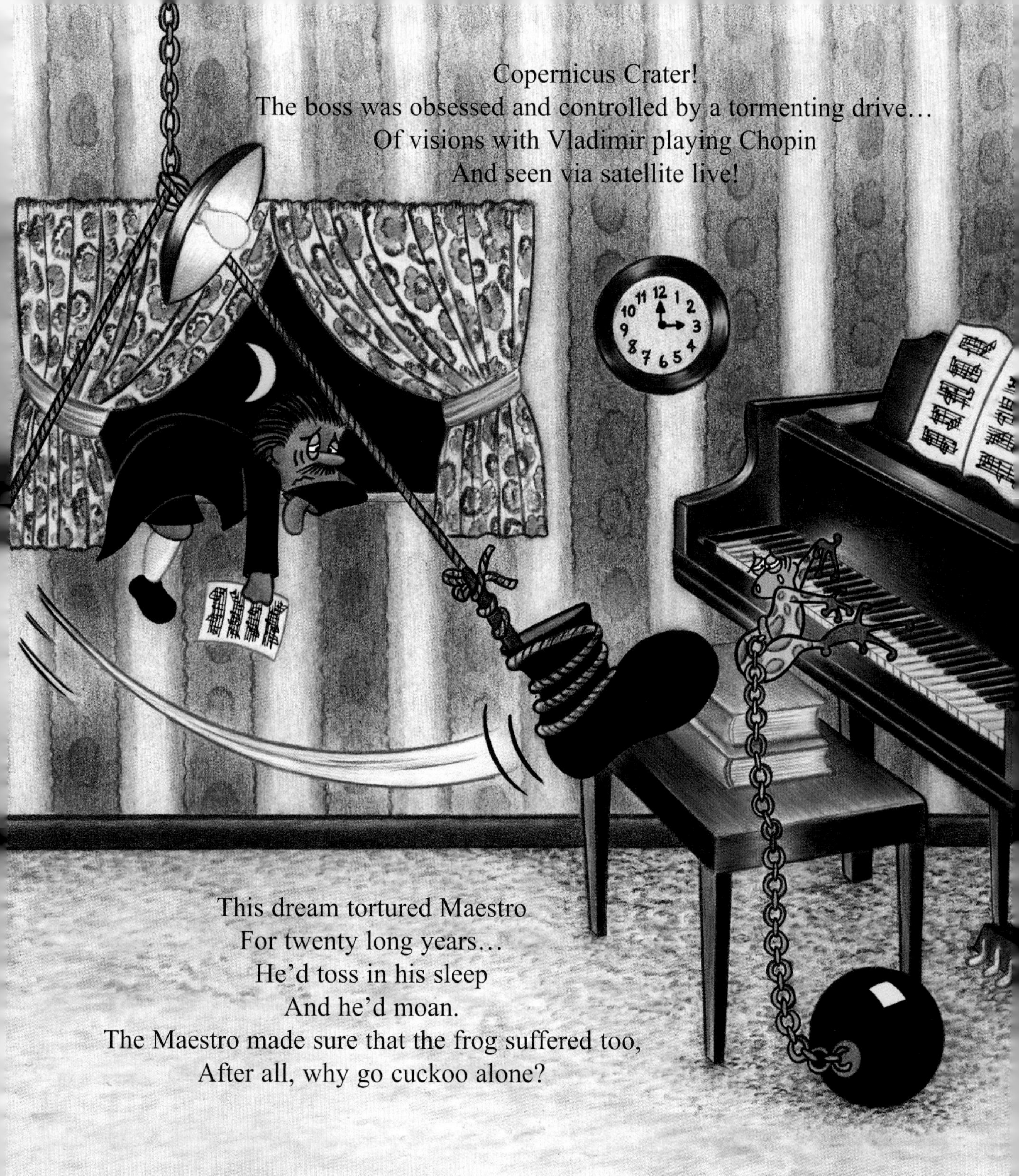

Copernicus Crater!
The boss was obsessed and controlled by a tormenting drive…
Of visions with Vladimir playing Chopin
And seen via satellite live!

This dream tortured Maestro
For twenty long years…
He'd toss in his sleep
And he'd moan.
The Maestro made sure that the frog suffered too,
After all, why go cuckoo alone?

Well, so long in coming, the day finally came. The concert was scheduled in May.
The **Big One** would be on the nineteenth long year
And three-hundredth and sixty-fourth day.

So just one day shy of twenty long years was Maestro's great moment to shine.
He grabbed the poor frog, and he shook him and said,
"Tomorrow it's all on the line.

"Pull this one off, and I'll see that you have an hour of sleep…a vacation.
I think you could use a long lazy snooze,
It's yours for a standing ovation."

To most of us, simply an hour of sleep is not what we'd call a big deal.
But for someone who hadn't had sleep twenty years,
The prospect held mighty appeal.

So Vladimir made up his mind then and there that he'd give it one thousand percent.
Still so naïve, he truly believed
That Maestro had said what he meant.

He'd *been* everywhere
And he'd *done* everything
That he'd been expected to do.
He honored his contract,
He never complained,
And now it was done. He was through.

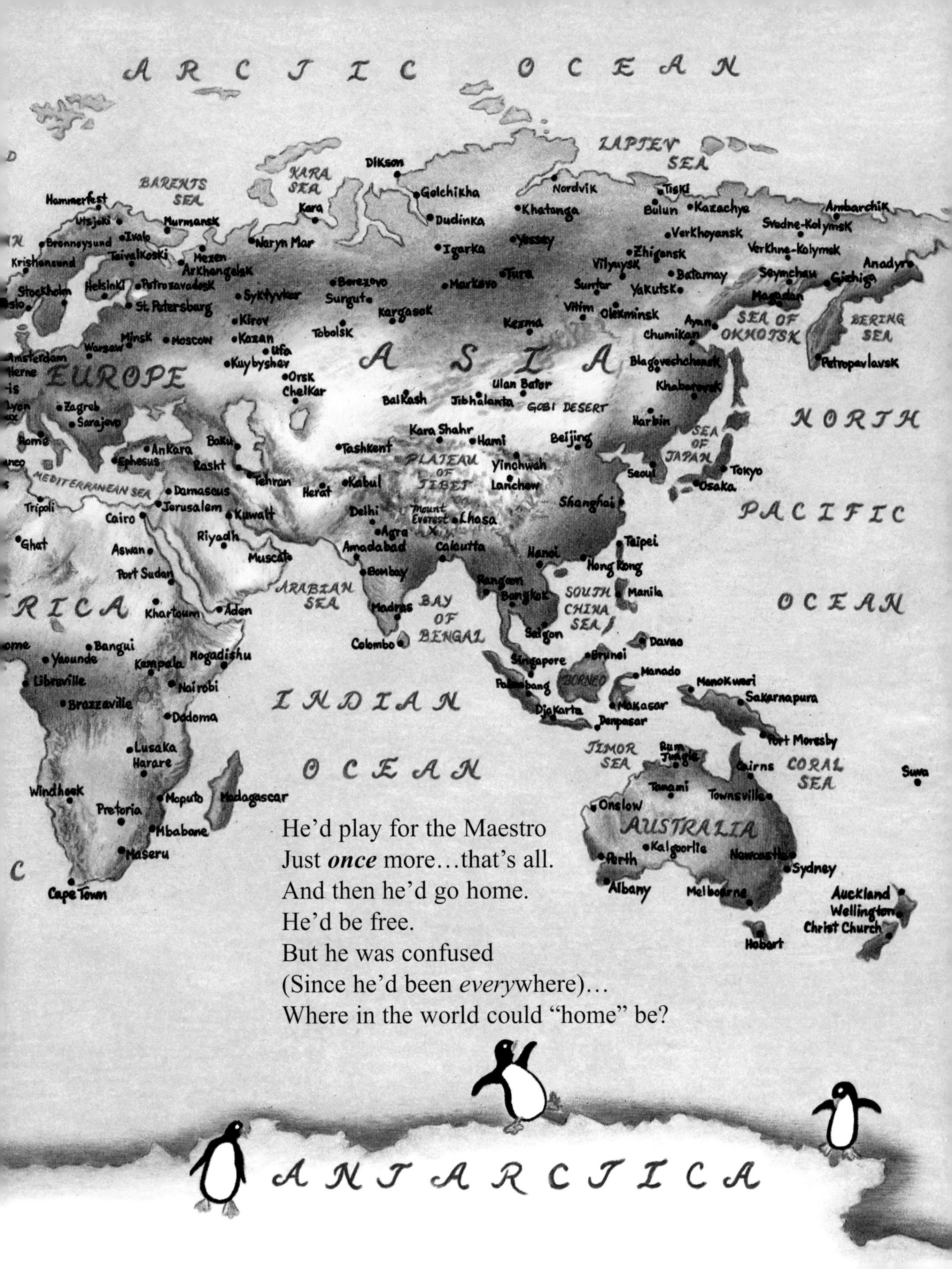

He'd play for the Maestro
Just ***once*** more…that's all.
And then he'd go home.
He'd be free.
But he was confused
(Since he'd been *every*where)…
Where in the world could "home" be?

Frenzied activity met them next day as paintings were auctioned and sold.
But really, great artworks were dullsville compared
To fingers and toes made of gold.
Though van Eycks, van Goghs, Rembrandts and Watteaus
Could be thought nothing short of magnificent…
Up against Vladimir, winner hands down, they really seemed quite...insignificant.

So quickly, mechanically, paintings were sold to just "get them out of the way."
In essence the people were there for one thing, and that was to hear the frog play.

They packed like sardines
In the great concert hall,
With murmurs that rumbled like thunder.

Breathlessly waiting, the crowd strained their ears
To witness this twenty-toed wonder.

And **THEN** it was time.

The lights were turned down, and one could have heard a pin drop.
The breathtaking Steinway on stage was the “cake”
And the frog was the “icing” on top.

Out on the stage, in tuxedo and tails,
His presence caused quite an uproar.
Victory meant sixty minutes of sleep
So he played like he'd never before.

9
8
7
6
5
4
3
2
1

This was the pinnacle of his career,
This was his moment to shine.
But Vladimir just saw himself all alone
Floating away on cloud nine.

Finally now maybe he could go home
And sleep like an underground mole.
But *where* he slept, that didn't matter so much…
No, home really wasn't the goal.
'Cause right now he couldn't care less if he slept
With a polar bear at the North Pole.

So as of that moment, the frog was released
From his contract, for it had run out,
But he was too valuable to let go of now,
Oh, Maestro would keep him…no doubt!

Promises, promises, right from day one,
But with everything he'd seen and heard,
Pepe knew Maestro had shown over time
That he wasn't a man of his word.

Pepe stood helplessly watching the crowd
As Vladimir took his last bow.
Sick to his stomach, he knew that the frog
Would *never* escape Maestro now.

Yes, Pepe knew it had only begun!
Maestro was mad for success.
The moon…but *then* what?
Saturn? Jupiter? Mars?
What followed was anyone's guess!

Pepe was desperate. He had to think fast.
Excitement and tension were mounting!
The moon would be next
And all systems were GO with the time:

MINUS 60 AND COUNTING

Vladimir was in a prison of sorts
And (so to speak) chained in a stock…
With eighty-eight keys at his fingertips and
Not *one* of them opened the lock!

ONE chance to give back the freedom on which
The Maestro was ever encroaching.

So with a deep breath,
Pepe snatched up some tape
As he saw the Maestro approaching.

Paintings were wrapped
And addressed on a pile
To be mailed one by one
From the stack…

And as one passed by,
Pepe grabbed Vladimir
And hastily taped him on back.

Not too much later
The frog was then found
To be missing,
And Maestro was frantic.

He had not a clue that his protégé was

Snoring high overtop the Atlantic.
(Proverbs 28:18)

So, that was what happened, so quickly it was
That Maestro and Vladimir parted,
The twenty long years in between is what dragged,
But it ended as fast as it started.

The rest of the story you may well have guessed…
The frog and this great masterpiece
Were mailed to the woods of the Weezies and then
They arrived at the home of…

…Maurice.

When Maurice untaped him

And tossed him outside,

Vladimir just crawled away…

And fell fast asleep on the very same rock where the Maestro first saw him that day.

Who would have known…the frog was back home…
For twenty years Vladimir missed it.
All for an offer he couldn't refuse,
Its pull was too strong to resist it.

Yes, quite a nightmare…and all of it real!
Perhaps a good time to wake up.
But give him a second; he'll sleep, after all,
He's got twenty years to make up.

“I’m not really sure,”
Nutmeg’s voice pierced his dream
And Vladimir woke from his doze.
“I’ll go to Dolly;
She ought to be home.
I’ll ask Dolly.
She always knows.”

“I’ve got a BETTER idea!” cackled Gus.
“Hey Vladimir! How about YOU?!”
He elbowed the frog once or twice in the ribs.
“You ought to know! What would YOU do?!”

"Sure, go ahead," the sleepy frog thought
As laughing, the pair skipped away.
"Paris, a bicycle…even the moon,
It's FREE…or at least so they say.

"However enticing an offer appears,
Do always with caution proceed.
And like an old sage, I'm so tempted to give
The advice you so desperately need.

"But, I guess there are things that are only well learned
Through a process of heartache and grief,
A journey for one that might take twenty years…
For another…it might be quite brief.

"I wish I could spare you that sorrow, my friends,
But it's something that's not meant to be.
You'd laugh if I told you, so no doubt until
You've walked it yourself you won't see.
I just only hope any lessons you learn
Are less painful than mine were for me.

"Don't jump into something too quickly because
You might find it's hard to undo.
It's just my opinion, but if you ask me…
Some things *are* too good to be true."

Items Of Interest

The word flaco is Spanish meaning "thin."

The Eiffel Tower is located in Paris, France.

The castle pictured is Vélez Blanco, located in southeastern Spain.
It was built in 1503 by Don Pedro Fajardo.

The Prado is a famous museum in Madrid, Spain.

Gazpacho is a cold, tomato soup.

The Iban, now a peaceful people, were once a feared headhunter tribe in Borneo.

Frederic Chopin was a famous Polish composer (1809-1849).

Famous Painters

Jan van Eyck (1390-1441)
Vincent van Gogh (1853-1890)
Rembrandt Harmenszoon van Rijn (1606-1669)
Jean-Antoine Watteau (1684-1721)

Steinway is a world famous piano with the distinctive reputation of being the best in the world, according to most concert pianists. It takes about one year to make a Steinway grand piano!

Jarrettsville is the home of Aunt Mugg.

Did you know...?

Apollo 11 was the first manned mission to land on the moon. The lunar orbiter transmitted live pictures back to earth of the first moonwalk on July 20, 1969. Neil A. Armstrong was the commander of the mission (and the first man to walk on the moon), Edwin E. "Buzz" Aldrin was the lunar module pilot, and Michael Collins was the command module pilot. Michael Collins orbited the moon while the other two astronauts walked on the moon's surface.

The moon is about 238,900 miles from the earth. Copernicus Crater is 58 miles in diameter and is on the side of the moon that always faces the earth.

The Sun is the center of our solar system. It is a big star, and if it were hollow, it could hold 1.3 million earths. The outer layer is called the photosphere and it is 11,000 ° F. The inner core is 27,000,000 ° F.

Planets

Mercury is closest to the Sun. It orbits the Sun in 88 days, and it takes 58 days to rotate one time. There is no atmosphere on Mercury.

Venus is the second closest to the Sun. It orbits the Sun in 225 days, and it takes 243 days to rotate one time. Venus is hotter than Mercury because its atmosphere traps heat.

Earth is the only planet known to sustain life. It orbits the Sun in about 365 days and takes 24 hours to rotate once.

Mars is called the red planet. It orbits the Sun in 687 days and takes 24 hours to rotate once. It is the fourth planet from the Sun. It has 2 moons.

Jupiter is the largest planet in our solar system. More than 1000 earths could fit inside of Jupiter! It takes 4332 days to orbit the Sun and less than half a day to rotate once. The great red spot we see is really a complex storm that moves on the planet. Jupiter has 16 moons.

Saturn is "the planet with the rings." It is the second largest in our solar system. It takes 29 ? years to orbit the Sun and only 10? hours to rotate once. Its density is 30% lighter than water, so if you could put Saturn in a swimming pool that was big enough to hold it, Saturn would float! Saturn has over 30 moons.

Uranus is the seventh planet from the Sun and the third largest. It takes 84 years to orbit the Sun and 17 hours to rotate once. Uranus has 22 moons.

Neptune takes 165 days to orbit the Sun and 16 hours to rotate once. Winds reaching 1,200 mph were measured on Neptune…the strongest ever recorded. Neptune has 8 moons.

Pluto is considered to be a dwarf planet. It is so small that Pluto and its one moon could fit inside the United States of America! It orbits the Sun once in 248 years, and it takes a little more than 6 days to rotate once. It is the farthest from the Sun and so it is very cold.

REFERENCED SCRIPTURES

The naïve believes everything,
But the prudent man considers his steps. (Proverbs 14:15)

The righteous is concerned for the rights of the poor,
The wicked does not understand such concern. (Proverbs 29:7)

He who walks blamelessly will be delivered,
But he who is crooked will fall all at once. (Proverbs 28:18)